Heidi

Look for all the
SCHOLASTIC JUNIOR CLASSICS

Alice in Wonderland
by Lewis Carroll

Gulliver's Stories
retold from Jonathan Swift

Heidi
retold from Johanna Spyri

The Legend of Sleepy Hollow
retold from Washington Irving

The Little Mermaid and Other Stories
retold from Hans Christian Andersen

Paul Bunyan and Other Tall Tales
adapted by Jane Mason

Robin Hood
adapted by Ann McGovern

Robinson Crusoe
retold from Daniel Defoe

The Wind in the Willows
retold from Kenneth Grahame

The Wizard of Oz
by L. Frank Baum

SCHOLASTIC JUNIOR CLASSICS

Heidi

Retold from
Johanna Spyri
by Sarah Hines Stephens

SCHOLASTIC INC.

New York   Toronto   London   Auckland   Sydney

Mexico City   New Delhi   Hong Kong   Buenos Aires

Copyright © 2002 by Sarah Hines Stephens.

Based on *Heidi* by Johanna Spyri, which was first published in 1880. All rights reserved. Published by Scholastic Inc. SCHOLASTIC and associated logos are trademarks and/or registered trademarks of Scholastic Inc.

ISBN 0-439-22506-X

12 11 10 9 8 7 6 5   4 5 6 7/0
Printed in the U.S.A.   40
First Scholastic printing, May 2002

Heidi

Chapter 1

IN a small Swiss town in the shadow of the mountains is a path that leads, straight and steep, into the Alps. At the base of it you can almost smell the fresh grass and fragrant flowers blooming farther up the mountainside. And if you happened to be there one morning in June you might have seen a woman making her way quickly up the trail, leading a small girl by the hand.

The woman did not stop to notice the flowers or the green grass. She had been up the path many times before. Besides, she was in a great hurry.

The small girl behind her struggled to keep up. Her cheeks flamed. It was no wonder. Though the June sun shone hotly down, the child was bundled up as if it were winter. She wore two or three dresses — one on top of the other, a red kerchief, and large wooden-soled shoes.

After an hour of steady climbing the pair came to Little Village. This was where Dete, the woman, had grown up. As they walked down the single narrow street, greetings rang out from nearly every cottage. But Dete did not slow her pace. She was not there for a visit.

Dete pulled the child through town without pausing. Soon they reached the far edge of the village.

"Wait a moment, Dete," a voice called from a cottage. "I'll walk with you up the mountain."

At last Dete paused. The little girl she'd been dragging along pulled her hand away and sat down on the ground.

"Are you tired, Heidi?" Dete asked.

"No, I am hot," the girl replied.

"It's just an hour more," Dete said encouragingly. Then she turned her attention to Barbel, the plump woman coming out of the cottage.

The two women linked arms and started up the path. They fell to talking like old friends. Barbel told Dete all of the news in Little Village. Dete told Barbel all about her life working in Baths. And the little girl, Heidi, trailed farther and farther behind.

"But Dete, you haven't told me where you are taking the child," Barbel said. "It's your sister's girl, isn't it? The orphan?"

"Yes, it is," Dete replied. "I am taking her to live with her grandfather."

"The Alm-Uncle? Have you lost your senses?" Barbel stopped on the path and stared at Dete. "He'll only send you right back down the mountain."

"He can't," Dete said plainly. "He *is* the girl's grandfather, and it is time for him to look after her. I've done it long enough. Besides, I've been offered a job in Frankfurt, and I can't keep Heidi with me."

"But what will the Alm-Uncle do with a child?" Barbel asked, shaking her head. "He has been living alone on the Alm for so long he's forgotten how to be civil. When he comes to the village he looks so angry everyone keeps their distance. People are afraid of him!" Barbel shivered and looked back to make sure the child hadn't overheard her.

But Heidi was nowhere to be seen.

Dete turned, too, and scoured the mountain.

"There she is," Barbel said after a moment. "She's found Peter and the goats."

Sure enough, Heidi was scampering over the rocks after Peter the goatherd and his flock.

"He's late this morning," Barbel remarked. "But it's no matter. Now he can keep an eye on her."

"Heidi doesn't need much looking after," Dete said as she continued up the path. "She may be only five, but she keeps her eyes open."

"Well, that's a good thing," Barbel said. She would have liked to add that Heidi wouldn't get much looking after from the Alm-Uncle, but she didn't.

At a small fork in the path the women parted. Murmuring something about the Alm-Uncle, Barbel turned left toward a run-down cabin. Dete waved good-bye and continued to the high hill where the Alm-Uncle lived.

Far below, Heidi could not see her Aunt Dete any longer. But she was not worried. She could still see the path. And anyway, she was much more interested in following the boy and the goats.

The blond boy sprang lightly over stones and crags. In his bare feet he was as nimble as his flock.

Now and then Heidi saw the boy look

back to see if she was still following him. It was hard for her to keep up in her hot clothes and clumsy shoes. Finally, Heidi sat down in a patch of grass and began to take them off.

First came the shoes. Then the kerchief and her dresses. Soon she was wearing nothing but a white cotton slip. Leaving the clothes in a heap, she dashed after the boy.

Heidi jumped from one rock to the next. She leaped over a bush, surprising the boy when she landed right beside him.

"I'm Heidi!" she exclaimed.

The boy was startled. He looked at Heidi's new outfit and the pile of clothes lying in the grass a ways off. His smile spread into a grin.

"I'm Peter," he said shyly.

"Are all of these goats yours?" Heidi asked.

"No, only one," Peter said. "I'm just the goatherd."

Heidi was very impressed. She had not met a goatherd before.

"Do you know my aunt Dete?" Heidi asked. She was beginning to wonder if she was still going in the right direction. Peter and his goats had wandered far from the path. He chose his own way up the mountain, taking the animals past the best bushes and shrubs.

"No," Peter said. "But if she was heading up the trail she must be going to see the Alm-Uncle. I'm on my way there, too."

Heidi followed Peter, running around with the goats. After a short while they rounded a turn. Dete was standing in the path with a hand on her brow. When she saw Heidi, her hand moved from her brow to her hip. She looked angry.

"Heidi, what have you been doing? Where are your clothes? And your new shoes?" Dete cried.

Heidi pointed calmly down the mountain. "There," she said. She could see the red kerchief, just a small red speck in the distance. "Don't worry, Aunt Dete, I don't need them."

Dete sighed. She looked at the pile of clothes and then at Peter. "Will you fetch Heidi's things for me?" she asked.

"I'm late already," Peter frowned.

"Here, then." Dete pulled a five-crown coin from her pocket. "You can have this coin when you get back."

Peter did not waste a moment. While Aunt Dete and Heidi continued up the path, he bounded down the mountain, with the goats running all around him. He quickly caught up with Heidi and Dete again, just as the Alm-Uncle's cabin was coming into view.

Chapter 2

THE Alm-Uncle's little house stood proudly on its cliff top. It was exposed to every bit of wind that swept the mountain and also every ray of sunshine. Behind the hut stood three tall fir trees. Off to one side was a smaller hut, as trim and tidy as the larger one.

The Alm-Uncle himself sat on a bench outside the door, chewing on his pipe. He watched Dete and the children make their way up the trail.

Heidi was the first to reach the hut. She went straight to the old man and held out her hand.

"How do you do, Grandfather?" she said.

"Well, well, what could this mean?" the old man said. But he did not smile.

Heidi was not afraid. She simply stared back at him without blinking. She had never seen anyone like her grandfather. He had a bushy white beard and gray eyebrows that met in the middle of his forehead like a thicket.

"Good morning, Uncle," Dete said, walking up behind Heidi. "I have brought you your grandchild. The child of your son and my sister."

The Alm-Uncle snorted. "Well, what am I to do with her?" Then he caught sight of Peter. He was standing behind Dete, watching to see what would happen. "And you there," he called. "You're none too early! Get along with your goats and take mine, too."

Peter whistled for his goats and ran off quickly. He did not want to make the Alm-Uncle angry.

"She's to stay with you, Uncle," Dete

said. She gave Heidi a small push closer to the old man. "I've looked after her for four years, and now it is your turn."

"Really?" the old man asked angrily. He stood up and his eyes flashed at Dete. "Suppose she begins to fret and whine? That is usually what happens with unreasonable little creatures. What shall I do with her then?"

"That is your business," Dete said.

The old man glared at Dete. His gaze was so terrifying that Dete took a step back. She wondered if she was right to leave poor Heidi with such a frightening man. But before she could change her mind, the Alm-Uncle pointed down the trail.

"Be gone, then, back to where you came from. And don't show yourself here again soon!" he growled.

Dete laid the bundle of clothes on the ground and hugged Heidi quickly. "Goodbye, Heidi," she said.

Then Dete turned and hurried down the path. She did not want her niece to see the tears in her eyes. She rushed down the mountain, straight through Little Village. She did not stop to talk to anyone. What if they asked after Heidi? "Poor child," they would say. "How could you?" they would ask.

Once she was on the train, Dete began to feel a little better. Soon she would have a good job and would be making more money. It would not be long before she could find a better home for the child.

Holding back her tears, she tried not to think of Heidi with the fierce Alm-Uncle as the train roared to Frankfurt.

Chapter 3

ONCE Dete had disappeared down the path, Heidi's grandfather sat back down on his bench. He blew great clouds of smoke with his pipe and kept his eyes fixed on the ground. He did not say a word.

Heidi had gotten a good look at her grandfather's eyebrows. Now she wanted to have a look around her grandfather's property. First she peeped into the small hut. It was empty. Then she circled the larger house and found the three tall fir trees.

As Heidi stood in the shade of the trees, a strong wind began to blow. It whistled and roared through the high branches.

Heidi stood very still and listened to the sound. It was like music.

When the wind stopped, Heidi walked around the rest of the house and found her grandfather sitting in the same place. She stood before him with her hands behind her back.

At last her grandfather looked up. "What do you want?" he asked.

"I want to see inside," Heidi replied.

"Come along, then." Grandfather rose. "Bring your clothes," he added, opening the cabin door.

"Oh, but I won't need those anymore," Heidi told him.

The old man turned and looked sharply at Heidi. The curly-headed girl rose on her toes. She was trying to get a look inside the cabin. Her eyes shone with curiosity. "Why won't you need them?" he asked.

"I'd rather go like the goats," Heidi said plainly.

"So you shall," Grandfather replied. "But bring your things so we can put them in the cupboard."

Heidi gathered her clothes. Her grandfather held open the door to the cabin, and Heidi stepped into a large room. On one side was a table and a chair. Grandfather's bed stood in one corner. In another was a fireplace with a kettle hanging in it.

Along the far wall was a large closet. Stacked neatly on one shelf were shirts and linens. Plates, cups, and silverware stood neatly on another shelf. A third shelf held a loaf of bread, some smoked meats, and cheese. Everything the Alm-Uncle needed.

As soon as the closet door was opened, Heidi rushed inside. She pushed her bundle into the far corner. Then she came back into the great room.

"Where shall I sleep, Grandfather?" she asked.

"Wherever you like," he replied.

Heidi was delighted. She looked into every nook and corner until she came to a small ladder. She climbed up and found herself in the hayloft. There was a fresh pile of sweet-smelling hay and a round window that looked down into the valley below.

"I will sleep here," Heidi called down. "It's beautiful! Come and see how beautiful it is, Grandfather."

"I know all about it," Grandfather shouted from below.

"I will make a bed," Heidi called. She rushed back and forth, gathering armloads of hay. "But I must have a cover. Do you have a cover for me to sleep on?"

Heidi made a neat little bed beneath the window so she could look out at the mountain.

"That bed is very nicely made," Grandfather said when he had climbed up into the loft. But before he put the cover over it, he gathered a huge armload of hay and made the bed twice as thick as it had been before. Then he helped Heidi place the heavy covering upon it.

Heidi looked at the cozy bed. "We've forgotten one thing," she said. "I need a blanket to crawl under."

"Is that so?" Grandfather asked. "And what if I haven't got any?"

"It's no matter," Heidi said. "I can use hay." She was about to gather up some more hay when Grandfather stopped her. He went down the ladder to his own bed and came back with a heavy linen blanket.

"Isn't this better than hay?" he asked as he spread it on top of the bed.

"It's perfect!" Heidi said. "I just wish it were night so that I could lie down."

"I think first we might have something to eat," Grandfather said. "What do you say?"

Heidi was so excited about her bed that she had forgotten everything else. Now she suddenly felt very hungry. It had been a long journey up the mountain and a long time since her breakfast of weak tea and toast.

The two climbed back down the ladder, and Grandfather pulled a three-legged stool up to the fireplace. He kindled a fire and hung a small kettle over it. Then he put a large piece of cheese on the end of a long fork. He moved it back and forth over the fire until it was toasted and golden.

Heidi watched with wide eyes. Then she had an idea and hurried to the closet.

When Grandfather brought the cheese and kettle to the table, he found that it had already been set with a round loaf of bread, two plates, two cups, and two knives.

"I see you can think for yourself," Grandfather said. "But there is something missing."

Heidi rushed back to the closet. There were only two glasses and one bowl left. These she gathered and brought back to the table.

"Very good," Grandfather said. "But where will you sit?"

Heidi raced across the room to the fireplace and pulled up the three-legged stool. Sitting upon it, her chin was barely as high as the table.

"It's a bit short, but the food is ready," Grandfather said. He filled a bowl with milk and placed it on his chair. Then he pushed the chair up to Heidi's stool, making her a little table. Next to the milk he laid a slice of bread and a large piece of golden cheese.

"Now, eat," Grandfather said. He sat down on the corner of the table.

Heidi picked up her bowl of milk. She drank without stopping. When it was gone she took a deep breath and set the bowl down.

"Do you like the milk?" her grandfather asked.

"It's the best milk I've ever tasted," Heidi answered.

"Then you must have more." Grandfather filled her bowl once more while Heidi tried the bread and cheese. They were as delicious as the milk.

When the meal was over Heidi followed her grandfather to his little shop in the back of the shed. He cut three thick sticks. Then he made a large circle from a board and cut holes into it. He put the sticks into the holes and turned it over.

"What do you suppose this is?" Grandfather asked.

"It is a stool for me," Heidi said, staring in amazement. "And you made it yourself!" Heidi clapped her hands and danced around her grandfather as he carried the stool inside.

As evening came the wind blew harder in the trees. The sound was so beautiful that Heidi had to rush outside and skip beneath the firs. Grandfather watched from the doorway as Heidi played. He smiled beneath his beard.

Heidi stopped her jumping only when she heard a shrill whistle in the front of the hut. She raced around the cabin to see goat after goat leaping down the mountain trail. Peter was with them. Heidi rushed to greet her friends from that morning, patting one goat after another.

When the flock reached the hut, two slender goats stepped away from the others and walked straight toward Grandfather.

"Are they ours, Grandfather? Are they both ours?" Heidi stroked each goat in turn. "Will they live in the shed and stay with us forever?"

"Go and get your bowl and the bread," Grandfather told Heidi.

When Heidi returned, Grandfather milked one of the goats, filling the bowl. He cut a piece of bread and handed the bowl and the bread to Heidi. "Eat your supper, and go up to bed. I must attend to the goats. Sleep well."

Heidi started to scamper inside. "Good night, Grandfather," she called. "Good ni —" Suddenly, Heidi turned around and raced out to the shed. "But Grandfather, what are the goats' names?" she asked.

"The white one is Little Swan, and the brown one is Little Bear," Grandfather replied.

"Good night, Little Swan. Good night, Little Bear," Heidi said loudly. Then she hurried inside to eat her supper.

When her meal was gone, Heidi climbed under her blanket and fell fast asleep. She slept so soundly in her cozy bed that she did not hear the fierce wind howling around the house.

Downstairs, Grandfather thought that Heidi might be afraid. After all, she was a small girl in a new place. He climbed the ladder and peered over the edge of the hay-loft. Moonlight shone through the round window onto Heidi's dark curls and rosy cheeks. Her mouth curved into a small smile, and she slept peacefully.

Grandfather gazed at the sleeping child until the moon went behind a cloud. Then he crept quietly back down to his own bed and went to sleep.

Chapter 4

HEIDI woke the next morning to a shrill whistle. She opened her eyes and saw the sun pouring in her window. It shined on the hay, making it look like gold.

For a moment Heidi was not sure where she was. Then she heard her grandfather's voice outside, and it all came back to her. Heidi jumped quickly out of bed, dressed, and scrambled down the ladder.

Peter and his flock were already outside. Little Swan and Little Bear were just coming out of their goat hut with Grandfather. Heidi ran over to wish them all good morning.

"Would you like to go climbing with Peter and the goats?" Grandfather asked. Heidi jumped for joy.

"Go and wash first, or else the sun will laugh at you." Grandfather pointed to a bucket of fresh water waiting by the door.

When Heidi had splashed and scrubbed herself shiny and clean, she scampered back to her grandfather. He was loading Peter's sack with extra food.

"Take good care," Grandfather said to Peter. "And give Heidi a bowl of milk at noon."

Peter nodded, and the whole flock started up the trail. Heidi skipped ahead with Little Bear, stopping here and there to look at the flowers. There were tiny bunches of pink blossoms growing by the rocks. The far hills were covered with dots of blue and specks of yellow.

Heidi picked flowers of every color and carried them in her skirt. She quickly darted here and there. Even Peter, who was used to keeping track of goats, sometimes had trouble finding her.

"If you pick them all there won't be any left for tomorrow," Peter laughed.

The flock continued up until they came to a meadow at the base of a high cliff. Here the goats nibbled on herbs and grasses as Peter stretched out in the sun to rest. Heidi put her flowers in the lunch bag and took a good look around.

The wide valley yawned below. Above, the jagged mountaintops stretched into the blue sky. Heidi sat very still, watching the wind play with the grasses and flower stems. She drank in the sunshine and felt happy.

Sometime later, a large blackbird circled high overhead. His piercing cry woke Peter, and he began to unpack their lunch.

While Peter milked Little Swan, Heidi jumped about with the goats.

"Stop your jumping, and come and eat," Peter called when Heidi's bowl was full of milk. Heidi was so excited that she could not eat all of the bread and cheese her grandfather had packed for her. When she had eaten her fill, she pushed the rest over to Peter. "You may have the rest. I am full."

Peter's eyes grew wide. He was not sure what to say. Never in his life had he been full enough to give food away. He was not sure he should take it.

"Please," Heidi said. "It's for you."

Peter smiled and took a bite. It was delicious. Soon his belly was as full as Heidi's. He settled back to watch Heidi play with the goats.

"What are the goats' names?" Heidi asked him.

Peter knew them all. Though he was only eleven, he had been herding the goats for several years. He collected them each morning in Little Village and took them home again each night. While Heidi darted back and forth among them, he called out the name of each goat.

There was Turk, who had big horns and was always butting the smaller goats. There was Fink, who was brave. He ran at Turk again and again, even though he was only half Turk's size. And there was also a little goat that would bleat and bleat so much that Heidi put her arms around her. That was Hopli.

"Why does she cry?" Heidi asked Peter.

"Because her mother was sold and doesn't come up the mountain anymore," Peter explained.

"Don't cry," Heidi told Hopli. "I will come up with you every day. Then you won't be lonely."

The little goat quieted and rubbed her head on Heidi's shoulder.

Of all the goats, Little Swan and Little Bear were the finest. Even Peter thought so. "They are the finest because the Alm-Uncle brushes them and washes them and gives them the best shed," he said with a nod.

Too soon the light began to change. The snow high on the hills turned rosy red and the blackbird returned to circle and cry. Peter started down the mountain. Heidi did not want the day to end. It had been perfect and beautiful, and she was sad to see it go. But she followed Peter and the goats down the mountain to her grandfather's house.

Grandfather was sitting outside his hut, waiting for the flock to return. Little Swan and Little Bear ran to see their master and lick the salt he held for them in his hand.

"Did you have fun, Heidi?" Grandfather asked.

"Oh, yes," Heidi told him. "I will remember what I saw today forever."

"But you can see it all again tomorrow," Peter said.

Heidi's heart leaped. She looked at her grandfather hopefully. "May I? May I really, Grandfather?"

"Of course." Her grandfather laughed.

"You can go up the mountain every day until winter."

Heidi jumped up and down. She hugged Little Swan and Peter and talked rapidly to her grandfather. "Oh, it is so wonderful up there," she cried. "There are so many flowers and a blackbird and snow on the mountaintops that turns red in the sunlight."

The Alm-Uncle smiled and pointed Heidi toward the water bucket. "Yes, yes," he said. "Now, why don't you go and wash. I'll fetch the milk, and you can tell me all about it over supper."

Chapter 5

EACH day Peter appeared as the sun rose. And each day Heidi and the goats went with him to the meadow.

The mountain air made Heidi strong and healthy. Her skin turned brown in the sun, and she was as happy as the birds in the trees.

When autumn came the winds began to blow louder and longer. They howled over the mountaintops until one day Grandfather told Heidi, "You must stay home today." He was afraid the wind would blow Heidi down into the valley like a leaf.

Peter was not at all happy. He enjoyed having Heidi with him in the meadow. He liked to share her lunch. And the goats always behaved themselves when she was there.

But Heidi was not very disappointed. She liked to go to the meadow with Peter. But she had as much fun staying home with Grandfather. She loved to watch him hammer and saw and prepare pretty round cheeses from Little Swan's milk.

More than anything Heidi delighted in the wind that blew in the fir trees out back. When she heard the rustle and roar of the wind in the trees she would drop what she was doing and run outside to stand beneath them.

The seasons continued to change. It grew cold, and Peter had to blow on his hands to warm them when he stopped at the Alm-Uncle's house to get the goats. Then one day Peter didn't come at all. It had snowed! The whole Alm was covered in a blanket of white. Not a single bit of green showed through.

Heidi watched the snow fall from her window. Thick flakes floated down for days on end. The snow got deeper and deeper until it almost covered the glass. But Heidi was snug inside Grandfather's cozy house.

When at last it stopped snowing Heidi's grandfather dug a path from the door. No sooner was he finished than there was a loud pounding and stamping outside.

It was Peter knocking the snow from his boots! He had climbed up the mountain to see Heidi.

"Good afternoon, Peter," Grandfather greeted him. "How is the general now that his goat army has deserted him? Are you busy pushing the pencil?"

"Why do you push a pencil?" Heidi asked.

"It's winter, and Peter must go to school," Grandfather said. "There he learns to read and write. Isn't that right, Peter?"

"That's right," Peter said glumly. "But

it's a lot of hard work. I would rather be with the goats."

Heidi had lots of questions about school. She and Peter talked all afternoon and warmed themselves in front of the fire. But soon it was time for Peter to go back down the mountain.

"I will come again next Sunday," he said on his way out the door. "And you must come and visit my grandmother sometime. I told her all about you, and she said you should come."

Heidi had never thought about visiting anyone before. She liked the idea very much. The very next morning she said to her grandfather, "I must go to the grandmother's today. She's waiting for me."

"Not today," her grandfather said. "It's too cold."

Heidi asked again the next day, and the next. Not a day went by that Heidi didn't say at least once, "I really must go to the grandmother's today. She's waiting for me to come."

"Come along, then," Grandfather said one day at last. He led Heidi to the shed and pulled out a wide sled. He sat down on it, and Heidi climbed into his lap. Then he wrapped a heavy blanket around Heidi and pushed off.

The sled shot down the mountain so fast Heidi almost thought she was flying. Before she knew it the sled had stopped in front of Peter's hut.

"Go on in," Grandfather said, unwrapping Heidi. "When it starts to get dark it is time for you to start home." Heidi nodded, and Grandfather began to pull the sled back up the hill.

Heidi opened the door to the little hut and went inside. The house had many rooms, but they were small and run-down.

Heidi walked through the kitchen and into a sitting room. She saw a woman mending Peter's jacket. Another, older woman sat in the corner. She was bent over her spinning.

"How do you do, Grandmother?" Heidi said. She walked up to the old woman. "I am Heidi. I hope you haven't been waiting too long."

The grandmother stared straight ahead. "Ah, the young girl staying with the Alm-Uncle," she said. She felt around until she found Heidi's hand. "Brigitte," the grandmother called to Peter's mother. "Come, tell me what she looks like."

"Let me open the shutter," Heidi said. "Then you can see me for yourself."

"The shutter is loose, child. It bangs and rattles like the rest of the house. But even if it were held open I could not see you," the grandmother said.

"Then we can go outside in the bright snow," Heidi said. She pulled gently on the old woman's hand.

"No, no, child," the grandmother protested. "There is no light in my eyes. I am blind and will never see again."

Heidi had never heard of such a thing. And she could not imagine not being able to see the beautiful mountain. She did not cry often, but suddenly she burst into tears.

The grandmother pulled the girl closer. "Come, dear Heidi," she said. "Don't cry. Let me tell you something. When a person cannot see they find it even more pleasant to hear a friendly word. It would make me so happy to hear you tell about your life with the Alm-Uncle."

Heidi dried her tears and began to tell the grandmother all about her life on the Alm. She spoke of the meadow and the trees. She told her about her grandfather's great skill with wood and a hammer. And how carefully he cared for his goats and made his cheese.

Suddenly, Heidi's story was interrupted by a thump at the door. Peter stomped inside. When he saw Heidi his face broke into a grin.

"Is that Peter? Home from school so early?" the grandmother asked. "How did the reading go?" she asked.

Peter hugged his mother and came to stand by his grandmother. "Just the same," he said glumly.

The old woman patted Peter's hand. "I only hoped there would be some change," she sighed.

"Why should there be a change?" Heidi asked. She did not know about reading.

"I only hoped that Peter might learn to read so he could read me the beautiful hymns in my book. It has been so long since I have heard them."

Brigitte handed Heidi the book that the grandmother was talking about. It was a book of prayers.

"Let me fetch a light so you can look at it," Brigitte said. "It's getting dark out."

Suddenly, Heidi remembered her promise to her grandfather and jumped up.

"Oh, no. I really must go," she said.

"So soon?" the grandmother asked. "The day has gone too quickly! Peter, go with her, and make sure she gets home safely."

Heidi said good night, and she and Peter pulled on their winter clothes. But before the children got five steps from the front door, the Alm-Uncle was there to meet them. He wrapped Heidi in a blanket, gathered her up in his arms, and started home.

Brigitte watched from the door of her hut and told the grandmother exactly what she saw.

"Thank the heavens that the Alm-Uncle is good to her," the grandmother said. "I hope he will let Heidi come and see me again."

Heidi was bursting to tell her grandfather all about the blind grandmother and their house. But the wind was howling. So she decided to wait until they were back inside Grandfather's cozy house. By the time they reached the hut she had an idea.

"Grandfather," she said excitedly, "tomorrow we must take the hammer and fix the shutter on the grandmother's house. We should take more nails, too. Everything creaks and rattles there."

"We must fix them?" Grandfather asked. "Who told you so?"

"Nobody told me," Heidi said. "I just know it, because everything is loose, and they cannot fix it themselves."

The old man looked at Heidi for a moment. "Then tomorrow we must," he agreed.

The next day Heidi and her grandfather flew down the mountain on their sled. While Heidi went inside to tell the grandmother stories, the Alm-Uncle fixed the loose shutter. He worked his way around the cabin, pounding in a nail here and a nail there. Before long he ran out of nails. But he came back the next day and the next. When he was finished, the cabin had stopped creaking and rattling entirely.

Chapter 6

THE seasons passed quickly on the Alm, and Heidi grew bigger and stronger. After two winters had passed, Peter's teacher sent word that Heidi should come to Little Village for school. But the Alm-Uncle knew that Heidi was happy on the mountain, and he did not want her to go. So he sent word back that Heidi would not be coming to school.

Heidi *was* happy. She loved her summers in the meadow and her winters by the fire. She was content to spend her time with her grandfather, Peter, Brigitte, the grandmother, and, of course, the goats. She did not long for lessons or the company of other children.

But one day a man came to visit the Alm-Uncle. When Heidi skipped out of the house she was startled to see him standing just outside the door. He was dressed all in black.

"Hello," he said. "You must be Heidi. Don't be frightened. I am an old friend of your grandfather's."

Heidi's grandfather came out of the little hut right behind her. He offered his hand to the man in black but did not look very friendly. "We were neighbors, once," Grandfather told Heidi. "What brings you up the path after such a long time, Pastor?" he asked the man.

"I think you know why I've come," the pastor replied. "It's about Heidi. I can see she's healthy and that you are taking fine care of her. But you must send the child to school."

Heidi's grandfather snorted and sat down on his bench. "She is thriving here with the goats and the birds. She learns only good things from them."

"She may learn good things, but she does not learn new things," the pastor said mildly. "She is not a goat or a bird. The time has come to send her to school with other children. Next winter she must begin schooling."

"I will not send her two hours down the hill in the snow and ice only to struggle two hours up at night. She's just a small girl. She could freeze." Grandfather knocked his pipe loudly on the bench.

"I agree. You should not send her out in the cold and the storms. Perhaps the time has come for you to return to the village as well." The pastor spoke gently. When he was finished the Alm-Uncle was quiet.

As he thought about what the pastor had said, the Alm-Uncle's eyebrows came down so far they nearly covered his eyes. After several moments he spoke. "You mean well, I know. But I will not send

Heidi to school in the village. Nor will I come down myself. Not next winter, not ever," he said as nicely as he could.

The pastor looked at his shoes. There was nothing more to say. So he turned and started down the path.

The rest of the day Grandfather was upset. When Heidi skipped up to him that afternoon his eyebrows were still lowered.

"Shall we go to see the grandmother?" she asked cheerfully.

"Not today," he said shortly. And he didn't speak for the rest of the afternoon.

Not two days passed before there was another visitor on the Alm. This time there was a knock at the door after breakfast. This time Heidi knew the visitor. It was her aunt Dete. She was dressed in a hat with feathers and a skirt that trailed on the ground.

Heidi opened the door wide for her aunt. The Alm-Uncle looked Dete over from top to toe but did not say a word.

Aunt Dete, though, had plenty to say. First she said how well Heidi was looking and how grateful she was that the uncle had taken such good care of her.

"I plan to take Heidi away," Aunt Dete told the Alm-Uncle. "I know having a little one must trouble you. And at last I have found a perfect situation for her. It's the best luck. I never would have thought that Heidi would be so fortunate." Dete spoke quickly and smiled at the Alm-Uncle's scowling face. When the Alm-Uncle said nothing, Dete went on.

"Some wealthy relatives of my mistress have a daughter who is not well and must spend all of her days in a wheelchair. She studies with a teacher but spends much of her time alone. She needs a study partner and playmate in the house. And the house is the finest in Frankfurt.

"They are looking for an unspoiled child, and, of course, I thought of Heidi," Aunt Dete rambled.

Heidi listened from her stool in the corner. She felt sorry for the girl her aunt spoke of. It would be terrible not to be able to run around like the goats.

Dete spoke faster and faster to fill the silence left by Heidi's grandfather. "Just think about the good luck. If something should happen to their only daughter — she is sickly — the family won't want to be childless, and they might just decide to keep —"

"Will you ever finish?" the Alm-Uncle interrupted.

Dete's smile disappeared. "You act as if I've just told you the most ordinary thing in the world. This is the best possible thing for Heidi and her future."

"Think what you like," the uncle snorted. "I will have none of it."

Dete exploded in anger.

"If that's what you think, Uncle, I will tell you what I think," she said sharply. "Heidi is eight years old. She can do nothing and knows nothing, and you will not send her to school to learn anything. I will not allow her to miss the opportunity that has been given her. If you go against me I am sure the people in Little Village will take my side. I daresay all of us know better than you what is right for a child."

"Silence," the uncle roared. There was fire in his eyes like Heidi had never seen before. "Take the girl, and be gone. I never want to see her with feathers in her hat and words in her mouth like the ones you have spoken to me today." With that the Alm-Uncle got to his feet and strode out of the house.

It took Dete a moment to find her voice. She turned to Heidi, who was not looking very happy herself. "Come now, get your clothes, and we'll be off."

"I will not come," Heidi said. "You've made my grandfather angry."

Dete sighed. "He'll soon be over it. And you don't know what you're saying. There are wonderful times in store for you in Frankfurt." Dete opened the closet and found Heidi's things herself. "Now, put your hat on. It is shabby, but it will do for today."

"I told you I will not come," Heidi said again.

"You're as stubborn as a goat," Dete said. She pushed the crushed straw hat down on Heidi's curls. "You heard your grandfather. He said we mustn't come into his sight again. He wants you to go with me. And you don't want to make him any angrier. Besides, you don't know how lovely it is in Frankfurt. You'll love it. If you don't, you can come back here. Perhaps by then your grandfather will be in better spirits."

"May I come back tonight?" Heidi asked.

"I said you can come home when you want to, didn't I? But first we have to get there. Tonight we'll stay outside Little Village, and tomorrow we'll be on the train."

Picking up the bundle of clothes, Dete took Heidi by the hand. Together they started down the mountain.

Peter was gathering rods for fishing when he saw Dete pulling Heidi down the path.

"Where are you going?" he called.

"To Frankfurt," Heidi answered. "But I must stop and see the grandmother first," she added. She tried to pull her hand away from her aunt. "She's expecting me."

"We're too late already," Dete replied. She did not loosen her grip. "You can see the grandmother when you come back."

Peter ran to his cabin as fast as he could. He threw his rods against the house.

"She's taking Heidi away," he cried to his grandmother.

Although Peter did not tell her, his grandmother knew it must be Dete who was taking Heidi away. She threw open her window. "Dete!" she cried. "Dete, don't take the child from us!"

But the grandmother's voice seemed to make Dete go faster.

Heidi pulled back as hard as she could. "The grandmother is calling. I must go."

"The sooner we get to Frankfurt, the sooner you can come back. And perhaps you can bring something for the grand-mother with you," Dete said.

This idea pleased Heidi, and she stopped pulling. "What can I bring her?" she asked.

"Something good," said her aunt. "Some soft white rolls would please her. She must have trouble eating black bread, it's so hard."

"Yes, she always gives her bread to Pe-ter," Heidi said thoughtfully. Soft white rolls were just what the grandmother needed.

"Let's hurry, then," Heidi said, spring-ing ahead. Now it was Dete who had to run to keep up. "If we hurry, perhaps I can be back with the rolls tomorrow!"

Heidi pulled her aunt quickly through

Little Village, without stopping. The people who saw them running through marveled at how well the girl looked after living with the Alm-Uncle. But she pulled so hard on her aunt's sleeve that everyone thought she was eager to leave the mountain. They had no idea that Heidi was only hurrying so she could return as quickly as possible.

Chapter 7

AFTER a long ride in a train and a short ride in a coach, Heidi and Dete arrived at the home of Herr Sesemann.

Heidi had never been in a house as large as Herr Sesemann's. But she wasn't allowed even a moment to look around. Dete pulled her quickly up the stairs behind the maid, Tinette.

"You are expected," Tinette said as she opened the door to the library. Dete gripped Heidi's hand tightly as a stern-looking woman rose to greet them.

Fräulein Rottenmeier, the woman in charge of the Sesemann house, gave Heidi a long, hard look. Her eyes rested on

Heidi's straw hat. "What is your name?" she asked finally.

"Heidi," she replied clearly.

"No, no. What is your given name?" Fräulein Rottenmeier asked impatiently.

"That is my name," Heidi answered.

Fräulein Rottenmeier shook her head and turned to Dete. "Is the child foolish or pert?" she asked.

"Begging your pardon," Dete said, "the child is neither. She means what she says, but she knows nothing of manners and has never been in a gentleman's house before. If it pleases you, the girl was baptized Adelheid."

"Well, that is a name with substance," Fräulein Rottenmeier nodded. "But, Dete, the child looks very young. Klara needs a companion her age to pursue her studies with. Fräulein Klara is twelve years old. How old is this child?"

"I don't recall exactly, but I think she must be ten, or nearly that," Dete replied.

"I'm eight," Heidi said helpfully. "Grand-father said so."

"Only eight!" Fräulein Rottenmeier exclaimed. "And what have you learned, child? What books have you studied?"

"None," Heidi answered honestly. "I don't know how to read, and neither does Peter."

Fräulein Rottenmeier looked stunned. "Dete, how could you bring me this creature? This is not what we discussed."

"The child is exactly what I thought the lady wanted," Dete said, standing tall. "She is unspoiled and quite different from other children. She fits the description perfectly. Now, if you will excuse me" — Dete began to back out the door — "I will come again soon to see how she is getting along." Before the fräulein could stop her, Dete had disappeared down the stairs.

Fräulein Rottenmeier rushed after Heidi's retreating aunt. She could see that Dete was determined to leave the girl.

But there were a few things she needed to discuss.

Heidi stayed where she was. She looked around the big room, filled with books, and noticed for the first time a girl who had been watching everything from her wheelchair.

The girl beckoned to Heidi from her spot in the corner. "I'm Klara," she said as Heidi approached. "Would you rather be called Heidi or Adelheid?"

"Heidi is the only name I know," Heidi told her.

"Then that is what I'll call you." Klara smiled. "I've never heard that name before, but it suits you perfectly. Tell me, did you want to come to Frankfurt?"

Heidi liked Klara. She saw no reason to tell her anything but the truth. "No," she said. "But tomorrow I shall go home and bring the grandmother some soft white rolls."

Klara giggled. "You're a funny one," she

said. "They've brought you to Frankfurt to stay and study with me. I can tell already it will make the hours go by much quicker. Herr Kandidat comes to teach me every day from ten until two. It can be very dull.

"Sometimes he holds a large book in front of his face. He pretends to be reading, but I know he is hiding a yawn. And sometimes Fräulein Rottenmeier raises her handkerchief and hides her whole face so it looks like she's been touched by the story we're reading. But she is yawning, too! Then I want to yawn so badly I can hardly stifle it, but I do. If I were to yawn they would say I was getting faint and make me take cod liver oil!

"I know it will be much more fun to study when you are there, too," Klara finished.

Just then Fräulein Rottenmeier came back into the library. She had not succeeded in catching Dete and was very cross. She snapped at Tinette, telling her to prepare Heidi a room. Then she barked at Sebastian, the butler, telling him to set another place at the table.

Tinette and Sebastian did not like to be yelled at. They went about their business as slowly as they could, which made the fräulein even more angry. But she could not say anything because she should not have yelled at them in the first place.

When the table was ready Sebastian came into the library to wheel Klara out. Heidi watched him closely as he crossed the room.

"You look just like Peter the goatherd!" she told him excitedly. Sebastian would have liked to ask about Peter the goatherd, but Fräulein Rottenmeier was scowling. She did not think Heidi should be talking to the servants and she would be angry with Sebastian if he spoke back. So the butler said nothing. But he gave Heidi a wink as he wheeled Klara out of the room.

Heidi took her place at the big table.

Next to her plate lay a lovely white roll. Heidi looked at it longingly. Sebastian came close to offer her some fish. Heidi pointed at the roll and whispered, "May I have that?"

Sebastian nodded. He had to bite his lip to keep from laughing when Heidi slipped the roll into her pocket.

Sebastian stood next to Heidi, holding his platter for a long time. Heidi had never had a servant before and did not realize that she should take some fish.

After a while Sebastian cleared his throat. Heidi quickly took some fish and put it on her plate.

"I can see I am going to have to teach you table manners," Fräulein Rottenmeier sighed. "And there are other things you will need to know as well." Fräulein Rottenmeier began listing instructions about getting up in the morning and going to bed at night. There were rules about shutting doors and coming in and going out. There were rules about orderliness in general and how to address the members of the household.

Heidi hardly heard a single rule. It was hard to focus with the fräulein sitting so far away at the end of the table. And the journey had been so long. Heidi suddenly felt very sleepy.

"Do you understand, Adelheid?" Fräulein Rottenmeier finally finished.

But it was Klara who answered. "I don't think she heard you," Klara giggled. For Heidi was fast asleep with her head next to her soup bowl.

Chapter 8

HEIDI awoke the next morning in a room with curtains on all of the windows. She had slept in a high white bed. At first she did not remember where she was. Then she recalled everything that had happened the day before and knew she was in Frankfurt. She even remembered some of the fräulein's instructions about getting up. Right away she sprang out of bed.

As soon as she was dressed Heidi ran to one of her windows. She wanted to see the sky and the grass. But the windows were so high that Heidi could barely see out at all. And when she did all she could see were walls. She rushed from one window to another, but the view was always the same. Walls and windows. Windows and walls.

On the Alm, Heidi could rush outdoors in the mornings to see if the sky was still blue and the sun was shining. She loved to stand on the mountain, listening for the murmuring trees.

Now she desperately wanted to open the window and put her head out. She wanted to see the green grass below and the snow melting high on the cliff. But no matter how hard she tried, the windows remained firmly closed.

Soon there was a knock at the door. It was Tinette the maid.

"Breakfast is ready," she said curtly. Then she closed the door again. Heidi wasn't sure what she should do. Tinette was so stern her words didn't sound like an invitation. Heidi sat down to wait and see what would happen. A few minutes later Fräulein Rottenmeier came in and saw Heidi sitting on her bed.

"What is the matter with you?" she asked. "Don't you know what breakfast means? Come down."

There was no mistaking what Fräulein Rottenmeier had said. So Heidi followed her down to the dining room. Klara was already waiting, with a warm smile for Heidi.

After breakfast Heidi followed as Klara was wheeled into the library. Together they waited for Herr Kandidat and the day's lessons.

"How do you see outdoors all the way down to the ground?" Heidi whispered to Klara while they waited.

Klara thought this was a funny question, but she did not laugh at Heidi. "We open the window and look out," she said.

"But the windows don't open," Heidi said sadly.

"Oh, Sebastian can help you open them!" Klara exclaimed.

Heidi was relieved to know that the windows opened. It made her room seem less like a cage. She decided she would ask Sebastian to open a window for her the next time she saw him.

Klara asked Heidi what she could see out of her windows at home. Heidi told her all about the Alm, her grandfather, the goats, and the meadow — everything she was fond of. She had only begun to tell Klara about the flowers when Herr Kandidat arrived.

Before the lesson, the teacher talked about Heidi with Fräulein Rottenmeier. She told him that Heidi had many things to learn, starting with her ABC's. She told him that she was sure Heidi was a stupid child. But Herr Kandidat knew that Heidi was not stupid just because she did not know the alphabet. He knew he could teach her many things.

Fräulein Rottenmeier slipped out of the library. She didn't know what to do with Heidi. It looked as though she was going to stay in Frankfurt. Fräulein Rottenmeier had hoped that Herr Kandidat would object to teaching Heidi. Then she would have a reason to send Heidi away. But Herr Kandidat thought it would be fun — and good for Klara, too — to have a younger child studying with them.

Suddenly, the fräulein's thoughts were interrupted by a terrible crash. Throwing open the library doors, she found Sebastian bending over an awful mess. There on the floor was a heap of books and papers. The tablecloth had been pulled across the room and ink from the inkstand was spilled the length of it.

Heidi was nowhere to be seen.

"That creature must have done this!" Fräulein Rottenmeier cried. She balled her hands into tight fists.

"It was Heidi," Klara said. "But you can't

blame her. She didn't mean to. She heard the carriages and was just in a hurry to see them. I don't think she's ever seen a coach before."

"See what I mean?" Fräulein Rottenmeier said to Herr Kandidat. "The child is unteachable. What will Herr Sesemann say to me if she has run away?" The fräulein dashed out of the library and down the stairs. Heidi stood in the open doorway, looking up and down the street.

"What is it, child?" the fräulein demanded. "Why have you run away?"

"I thought I heard the wind in the fir trees," Heidi said. "But I don't know where they are, and I don't hear it any longer." Heidi looked down the street.

"Firs! We are not in the woods! Now, come see what a mess you have made." Fräulein Rottenmeier made her way back up the stairs. Heidi followed.

Heidi was surprised to see the mess on the floor. She had been in such a hurry to see the trees that she hadn't noticed she was dragging the tablecloth with her.

Tinette and Sebastian quickly put the room back in order. Heidi sat very still for the rest of the lesson. And Klara didn't have to stifle even a single yawn!

In the afternoon Klara took a long rest, and Heidi was allowed to do what she pleased. She was glad to have some time to herself. She had been working on a plan all morning and was sure it would work.

Heidi sat down in the middle of the hall outside the dining room and waited. Sure enough, Sebastian came walking by, with a tray full of silver.

Heidi stepped up to him and tugged on his sleeve. "I would like to ask you something," she said. "And I'm sorry about this morning," she added. Sebastian had been responsible for getting the ink out of the carpet.

"Go ahead, mam'sell," Sebastian said, putting down his tray.

"My name isn't Mam'sell," Heidi said. "It's Heidi."

"Yes, but Fräulein Rottenmeier asked me to call you so," Sebastian explained.

"Well, then, now I have three names," Heidi sighed. For she had already noticed that whatever Fräulein Rottenmeier wanted, she got.

"What did little mam'sell want to ask?" Sebastian said. He set the tray down and began to put away the silver.

"How do you open the windows?"

"This way," Sebastian said. He pushed up a large one.

Heidi went to the window and tried to see over the edge. Sebastian brought her a stool to kneel on, and she leaned way out.

"Now you can see," Sebastian said.

"But there's nothing but a stony street," Heidi said disappointedly. "If you go clear around the house to the other side, what do you see there?" she asked.

"Just the same," Sebastian answered.

"But where do you go to see across the valley?"

"You have to climb high in a church tower, like the one with the golden dome there." Sebastian pointed out the window. "From there you can see a great distance."

Heidi thanked Sebastian and climbed down from the stool. She rushed downstairs and out the door. But she did not find the church steeple just outside as she imagined she would.

Heidi walked to the end of one street and another. Still she was not at the steeple. She asked people along the way. Some were able to point her in the right direction, and at last she came to the church. She stepped up to the door and rang the bell.

"What do you want?" an old man asked when he answered the door.

"I want to climb the tower," Heidi said.

"What do you want up there?" the man asked. "You'll have to come back with your parents. I don't have time for this."

"I want to go up so I can look down," Heidi said. "Please, just this once."

The old man looked down into Heidi's pleading face. "Very well. Come with me," he said in a kinder voice. He offered Heidi his hand.

Holding the tower keeper's hand, Heidi climbed step after step. The stairs grew smaller and smaller, until at last they reached the top. The keeper lifted Heidi up to the open window.

Heidi saw below her a sea of rooftops, towers, and chimneys, but there was no valley. There were no mountains and trees.

"It's not at all what I thought it would be," she said, disappointed.

"Is that so?" the keeper snorted. "Well, what does a young girl like you know?" He stomped back down the narrow steps, with Heidi behind him.

When they passed the keeper's room, Heidi saw a basket with a large gray cat in it. The cat growled and Heidi stepped back.

"She has kittens," the keeper explained. "Come have a look."

Giving the cat a reassuring pat, the keeper crouched near the basket. Heidi got closer and cried out in delight when she saw the kittens. She sat on the floor and laughed as the tiny creatures crawled and jumped and tumbled over one another.

"Would you like one?" the keeper asked.

"For my own? To keep?" Heidi asked. She could not believe her good luck.

"You can have more than one if you like," the keeper laughed. He needed to find homes for the whole litter.

"I can keep one and take one to Klara!" Heidi clapped her hands together. The keeper held the mama cat while Heidi chose two kittens, a pure white one and a playful one with yellow stripes.

Heidi carefully put one kitten in her right pocket and the other in her left. Then she thanked the keeper and made her way back to Herr Sesemann's house.

Chapter 9

HEIDI reached up to ring the bell, with the kittens still in her pockets. But before she could reach it, Sebastian opened the door.

"Quick, mam'sell!" Sebastian urged. He pulled her inside. "Go right in to the table. They are all waiting, and Fräulein Rottenmeier looks like a loaded cannon!"

Sebastian pushed Heidi into the dining room and followed her in. The fräulein did not look up. Klara did not say anything, either. The silence was terrible.

When the fräulein spoke, it was even worse. "Adelheid, you have behaved very badly," she said sternly to Heidi. "Leaving the house without permission and wandering the streets is not allowed. I've never heard of such conduct. Do you have anything to say for yourself?"

Heidi opened her mouth to speak.

"Meow," was the reply.

"What?" Fräulein Rottenmeier grew angrier. "Do you dare to be rude?"

"But I didn't —" Heidi began.

"Meow, meow."

A strange look came over Sebastian's face. He put down his tray and rushed out of the room.

"That is enough!" Fräulein Rottenmeier screeched. "Adelheid, you may go to your room!"

Heidi felt very frightened. She had never seen anyone as angry as the fräulein.

"I really didn't —" she tried to say.

"Meow, meow, meow!"

"Oh, Heidi," Klara spoke up, "you can see how angry you are making Fräulein Rottenmeier. Why do you keep saying meow?"

"I'm not. It's the kittens," Heidi finally explained without interruption.

"What? What?" Fräulein Rottenmeier shrieked. "Kittens? Sebastian! Tinette! Find the horrible creatures, and take them away. Now!"

Sebastian was standing just outside the door, trying not to laugh. He had seen a kitten poke out of Heidi's pocket while he was serving dinner. When it began to cry he could hardly contain himself long enough to leave the room.

When Sebastian stopped laughing and finally went back in, everything was peaceful. The fräulein had gone to the library. She was terrified of cats.

Klara held the two kittens in her lap, and Heidi knelt beside her. They were delighted with the fuzzy creatures.

"Sebastian," Klara called, "you must help us. Can you find a bed for the kittens where the fräulein won't find them? We want to keep them and we'll only bring them out when we're alone. Isn't there someplace you could put them? Please?"

"I will take care of them," Sebastian assured her. "I will make a fine bed in a basket and put it someplace safe." Sebastian lifted the kittens out of Klara's lap with a smile.

Sebastian left the dining room, still smiling. He was happy to help with the kittens. He secretly enjoyed seeing Fräulein Rottenmeier upset. She was too cranky too often.

Fräulein Rottenmeier didn't come out of the library until after bedtime. So for the moment Heidi was spared her punishment. Both she and Klara went to sleep happily, knowing their kittens had a cozy bed of their own.

The next day the fräulein was still angry. "Today I will decide your punishment, Adelheid," she announced at breakfast.

"Oh, no!" Klara protested. "We must wait for Papa. He will know what to do."

Fräulein Rottenmeier did not look pleased to hear Klara's father's name. "Very well, Klara," she said through tight lips. "We will wait for Herr Sesemann."

The days that followed were peaceful. Klara was happy. Her lessons were no longer dull. And in the afternoon Heidi would tell Klara all about her life on the Alm.

Heidi loved to talk of the mountain. But sometimes her happy stories made her feel so homesick she began to cry. "I really must go home," she would sob. "Tomorrow I must go home!"

Klara always calmed her down. "Wait," she told the younger girl. "Wait until Papa comes. Then we shall see."

More than anything, Heidi longed to be on the Alm. She consoled herself with the thought that every day she stayed she added two more rolls to the basket for the grandmother. Every day at lunch and at dinner she slipped the soft white bread into her pocket. Later she tucked it into the closet in her room. Thinking of all of those rolls made Heidi feel a little better.

Then one afternoon her longing was too much. Klara was sleeping, and Heidi had been forbidden to talk to Sebastian. So she packed up her basket of rolls and put on her kerchief and battered straw hat. She was almost out the door when she ran into Fräulein Rottenmeier, who was coming in.

"What's this?" the fräulein cried. She eyed the basket and shabby hat. "Are you trying to go out on your own again after the trouble you got into last time?"

"I'm not going out. I'm going home," Heidi replied matter-of-factly.

"Home? You are running away from Herr Sesemann's house? I won't hear of it!" the woman raged. "Aren't you treated better than you deserve? Have you ever in your life had a room or meals or service like you have here? Tell me!"

"No," Heidi replied truthfully.

"You see? You have everything you need. You are an ungrateful child."

Heidi fought back the tears welling up in her eyes. "But I must go home," she said. "I have been away so long. Hopli must be crying on the hill. The grandmother is expecting me. And Peter must be hungry for more cheese."

"The child is crazy!" Fräulein Rottenmeier exclaimed. "Sebastian! Bring the child upstairs at once!"

Sebastian came quickly down the stairs, almost bumping into the fräulein as she rushed up. When he saw Heidi trembling in the doorway, he spoke gently.

"What have you been up to now?" he asked.

Heidi made no reply. She didn't move when Sebastian touched her arm.

"Come now," Sebastian urged. "You must be brave and happy. That's the best way. Would you like to visit the kittens? They are happy and play all the time."

At last Heidi nodded. But it was a small nod, and she looked so sad Sebastian's heart nearly broke as he led the girl to her room.

All during supper Fräulein Rottenmeier cast sharp glances at Heidi. It was almost as if she expected her to do something terrible. But Heidi sat still as a mouse. And after slipping her roll into her pocket she didn't touch her food.

After supper the fräulein seemed to have a new mission. Herr Sesemann was coming home soon. She was worried that he would think she wasn't looking after Heidi properly.

First the fräulein told Klara to give Heidi some of her old things. Klara thought that was a fine idea. But when the fräulein went to Heidi's closet to decide what should be kept and what should be thrown out, she was met with a surprise.

"You can't imagine what I've found," she exclaimed as she burst in on Klara and

Heidi's lesson. "There is bread in your closet, Adelheid. A huge pile of bread! Who has heard of such a thing? Tinette! Take away the bread in Adelheid's closet. Take the straw hat, too. Toss them both away."

"No!" Heidi cried. "I must have the hat, and the rolls are for the grandmother!"

Heidi tried to rush after Tinette, but Fräulein Rottenmeier held her fast. "You will stay here where you belong. That rubbish will be taken away and put where *it* belongs."

Heidi collapsed onto her knees next to Klara's chair and began to cry. The fräulein, who did not know what to do with crying children, left the room.

"Now the grandmother won't have any rolls. They were for the grandmother, and now they're gone. She won't have any," Heidi sobbed.

"Heidi, don't cry," Klara tried to comfort her friend. "I promise I will give you just as many rolls when you go home. And they will be fresh and soft. The rolls you had would be hard by the time you got them home. Please, Heidi, don't cry."

It was a long time before Heidi could stop crying. "Will you really give me bread for the grandmother? Just as many as I had?"

"Of course," Klara said.

Heidi felt a little better. And that night when she went to bed, she felt better still. For there, hidden under the cover, she found her crumpled straw hat.

Chapter 10

A FEW days after Heidi tried to go back to the Alm, there was a great bustling in the Sesemann house. Sebastian, Tinette, and Johann, the coachman, hurried up and down the stairs. Herr Sesemann, Klara's father, had come home!

When he arrived, the first thing the gentleman did was go straight to his daughter's room.

"Papa!" Klara cried when she saw him. Herr Sesemann rushed to Klara's side and hugged his daughter close. When he had gotten a good look at her and seen that she was looking well, he held out his hand to Heidi.

"You must be our little Swiss girl," he

said kindly. "Now, tell me, are you and Klara friends?"

"Oh, yes," Heidi answered. "Klara is always good to me."

"I'm glad to hear it," Herr Sesemann said. "And I want to hear more. But now I must get some lunch and talk to our Fräulein Rottenmeier. She said she has something urgent to discuss."

Fräulein Rottenmeier was waiting for Herr Sesemann. She sat in the dining room, with a scowl on her face.

"Fräulein Rottenmeier," Herr Sesemann said when he saw her, "what can be the matter? Why do you look so cross? Klara seems very well."

"Herr Sesemann," the woman began seriously, "I know you only want your Klara to associate with good people. I'm afraid we have been fooled by the companion we have chosen for her."

"Fooled?" the master asked.

"She has filled the house with wild animals and strange ideas while you were away."

"Animals?" Herr Sesemann asked. He was more amused than worried. "What are you talking about, Fräulein?"

"I cannot understand the child at all. I think she may be out of her mind," Fräulein Rottenmeier went on. She folded her hands on the table.

Herr Sesemann looked closely at the fräulein. It was almost as if he was trying to decide if *she* was out of her mind. Then he left the room to speak with his daughter. After sending Heidi to the kitchen for some water, Herr Sesemann knelt again by Klara's chair.

"Now, my dear," he said as he took her hand, "what is this about animals in the house? And why does Fräulein Rottenmeier think your companion is not suitable?"

Klara saw that her father was very serious. But when she had finished telling

him about the kittens and the rolls Heidi
had hidden in her closet, Herr Sesemann
laughed heartily.

"So you don't want me to send her
home? You are not tired of her?"

"Oh, no, Papa! Don't send her home,"
Klara begged. "Since Heidi has been here
something fun happens every day. Time
goes so quickly now. Not at all like before.
And Heidi tells me so many wonderful
things!"

Herr Sesemann patted Klara's hand.
"Very good," he smiled.

The next day, when Klara was resting,
Herr Sesemann asked Fräulein Rottenmeier where Heidi spent her afternoons.

"She sits in her room, though she ought
to busy herself with something useful.
That is probably where she makes up her
absurd plans," the woman replied.

"That is precisely what I would do if I
was trapped in a room," Herr Sesemann

commented. "Bring her to me. I want to give her some books."

"That child can't do anything with books!" Fräulein Rottenmeier exclaimed. She wrung her hands. "She has been having lessons for weeks and still does not know her alphabet!"

"How strange," Herr Sesemann said thoughtfully. "She seems like a clever child."

Fräulein Rottenmeier looked like she wanted to say something. But she remained silent as she turned to fetch Heidi.

Heidi was thrilled with the books Herr Sesemann showed her. She had never seen such big, bright pictures before. She turned page after page carefully. Then she came to a picture that made her breath catch in her throat. Tears sprang to her eyes, and she quickly wiped them away. She knew that crying made Fräulein Rottenmeier angry, and she did not want to anger Klara's papa.

Herr Sesemann saw Heidi linger over the picture of a green meadow. Animals were grazing, and in the middle stood a shepherd, leaning on a staff.

"Tell me, Heidi, do you like your lessons?" Herr Sesemann asked.

Heidi tore her eyes from the picture. "Yes," she nodded.

"Are you studying well and learning to read?"

"Oh, no," Heidi said. "But I knew that couldn't be learned. It's too hard."

"How do you know that?" Herr Sesemann asked.

"Peter told me," Heidi said. "He knows because he has been trying for so long. But he has never learned because it is too hard."

"Let me tell you something," Herr Sesemann said gently. "You have not learned to read because you believe Peter. Now I want you to believe me. I am telling the truth when I say that you can learn to read, and in a very short time. Many children do. And when you do, you will be able to read all about the shepherd in the green meadow. You would like that, wouldn't you, Heidi?"

Heidi had been listening very carefully. "Oh, yes," she said. Her eyes sparkled. "If only I could read now!"

"It will come," Herr Sesemann said. "And it won't take long. I can tell that already."

From that day on Heidi paid close attention to Herr Kandidat. She learned very quickly. And one night at dinner she came downstairs to find the beautiful book with the picture of the shepherd sitting on her plate.

Heidi looked eagerly at Herr Sesemann.

"The book belongs to you now." Herr Sesemann nodded.

"Forever?" Heidi asked. "Even when I go home?"

"Yes," the gentleman said.

Heidi beamed. After dinner, she read Klara the story of the shepherd. That night when she went to bed, she took the book with her into her room. And from that night on Heidi sat with the book whenever she could and read all of the stories many times. But her favorite was always the one about the shepherd.

Chapter 11

THE days passed quickly while Herr Sesemann was home, but all too soon it was time for him to leave again. With her new book, Heidi felt happier than she had in some time. But ever since Fräulein Rottenmeier had told her how ungrateful she was, there had been a change in Heidi. She now understood that she could not go home when she wished. She knew she must stay in Frankfurt for a long time. Perhaps forever.

Heidi thought about going home all the time. But she stopped talking about it. She did not want Herr Sesemann and Klara to think she was ungrateful.

As the days and weeks went by, Heidi's

heart grew heavier and heavier. She could barely eat. She grew pale. At night, when she fell asleep, she would dream of the Alm. She would see the green grass and the mountain peaks. She would awake full of joy, ready to run out of the hut and throw her arms around Little Swan and Little Bear. But she couldn't. She was in her big bed in Frankfurt, far away from the Alm.

With Herr Sesemann gone, the house grew quieter. Heidi spent even more of her time reading. Sometimes she read aloud to Klara. One day she was reading a story about a dying grandmother when she suddenly began to cry.

"The grandmother is dead!" Heidi sobbed. The story seemed so real that Heidi was sure the grandmother on the Alm had died.

Klara did her best to comfort Heidi. She explained that the grandmother in the story was entirely different from the grandmother on the Alm. But still Heidi kept crying.

Heidi had never realized that something bad could happen to the grandmother on the Alm — or to her grandfather — while she was away. She could not bear the thought of something happening to them.

Heidi continued to sob loudly. Soon Fräulein Rottenmeier came in to see what the fuss was about.

"Adelheid, we have had enough of your useless screaming," she said sternly. "If there is ever such an outbreak again while you are reading I will take your book away and you won't get it back."

Heidi choked back her tears. She turned ghostly white. The book was her dearest treasure. From that moment on Heidi was careful not to let anyone see her cry. But she often wept softly into her pillow when everyone else was asleep.

Chapter 12

FOR several days Fräulein Rottenmeier had been acting strangely. When she walked around the house in the evening she looked quickly into dark corners. Now and then she looked back as if she thought someone was following quietly behind her. If she had to go upstairs or down into the great hall, she asked Tinette to go with her.

Oddly, Tinette did the same thing. When she had work to do upstairs or down she called on Sebastian, telling him that she might need him to carry something.

Stranger still, Sebastian would call on Johann when he was sent to the far corners of the house. "I might need your help," he told him. Rarely did anyone need help, but everyone followed willingly just the same. They all knew that something strange was going on in the Sesemann house.

For every morning the servants found the front door standing wide open. Nobody could explain why.

The first few times this happened they thought a thief had broken in. Sebastian and Tinette searched the house to see if anything had been stolen. But not a single thing was missing.

Every night the door was double locked. There was even a wooden bar placed across it. It made no difference. Every morning the door stood open.

It seemed the Sesemann house was haunted.

At last, at Fräulein Rottenmeier's request, Johann and Sebastian worked up the courage to investigate. They gathered everything they needed and prepared to sleep that night in the room adjoining the great hall.

At first the two men talked easily. But after a while they settled back in their chairs and grew quiet. They soon fell asleep, but when the town clock struck twelve Sebastian jerked awake. It was very dark and the hall was silent. Sebastian called to Johann and tried to wake him, but Johann was fast asleep.

At one o'clock it was Johann who was startled awake. He sat up in his chair.

"Sebastian," he called, "we mustn't be afraid. We must go and check on things. Follow me."

Johann opened the door to the great hall. A gust of cold air rushed in and blew out the candle Johann was holding. The cold air woke Sebastian, who stood up quickly. But when Johann came running back into the room, Sebastian was knocked

back down. Johann slammed the door behind him and quickly turned the key in the
lock. He was trembling like a leaf.

Sebastian relit Johann's candle as fast as
he could. When he saw Johann's face, he
nearly cried out. It was ghostly white.

"What is the matter? What did you see?"
Sebastian asked.

"The door was wide-open, and there
was a white form on the steps. It walked
toward me!" Johann gasped.

Cold shivers ran down Sebastian's back.
There was a ghost in Herr Sesemann's
house!

The two men sat close together until
morning. Then they walked carefully out
of the room, closed the front door, and
went upstairs to tell Fräulein Rottenmeier
what had happened.

Fräulein Rottenmeier did not waste any
time. As soon as Sebastian and Johann
stopped talking, she wrote a letter to Herr

Sesemann. Afraid for the lives of everyone in the house, she begged him to come home immediately.

Herr Sesemann replied quickly. He was sorry for the strange happenings, but he could not leave his business. He was sure that there was no real reason to be afraid and was certain that Fräulein Rottenmeier could handle things on her own.

Fräulein Rottenmeier was not pleased. She thought Herr Sesemann should come home at once. She had not yet told the children about the ghost. She did not want them to be afraid and have trouble sleeping. If they were, they might insist that she stay with them every moment. But even that was better than dealing with a ghost. She called them both into the parlor and told them everything.

It was not long before Klara began trembling in fear. "I will not stay alone in the house for a moment!" she sobbed. "Papa must come home!"

Klara did not stop crying until Fräulein Rottenmeier promised to write to her father again. She also agreed to move her bed into Klara's room. The fräulein offered to have Tinette move into Heidi's room. But Heidi was more afraid of stern Tinette than any ghost, so she declined.

When Klara was calm, Fräulein Rottenmeier wrote again to Herr Sesemann. She told him that the mysterious goings-on were having a terrible effect on his daughter's health.

Two days later, Herr Sesemann arrived at his front door. He did not stop to talk to the servants or to remove his coat. He went directly up to Klara's room.

"Papa!" Klara cried when she saw him. She looked so happy and well that the stern look on Herr Sesemann's face quickly disappeared.

"If the ghost has brought you home, then I am happy about the haunting," Klara told her father.

Herr Sesemann was not happy that he had been fooled, but a small smile played on his lips when he asked Fräulein Rottenmeier if the ghost had been up to any more pranks.

"It is no laughing matter," Fräulein Rottenmeier replied solemnly. "You shall soon see."

Herr Sesemann was sure that the ghost was really the work of a human and went to the pantry to find Sebastian. "Have you been playing the part of the ghost to scare Fräulein Rottenmeier a little? Tell me. I won't be angry."

"No, sir. On my word," Sebastian replied. "Johann saw the ghost in the night, and I nearly did myself."

"Tomorrow you will both see the ghost in daylight," Herr Sesemann chuckled. "Now, please go and fetch my friend Dr. Classen. Tell him I have come home unexpectedly and need him to sit with me through the night."

Sebastian did as he was told. That night, when the children had gone to bed and Fräulein Rottenmeier had retired, the doctor rang the bell.

At first Dr. Classen was concerned that his old friend was sick. But he laughed heartily when he saw that Herr Sesemann was in good health. "You don't look at all like someone who needs to be watched through the night!" he declared.

"Not me, Doctor. Not tonight. Tonight we will be watching for ghosts!"

Herr Sesemann explained to the doctor about the hauntings. Then the two settled into the same chairs that Sebastian and Johann had kept watch from the week before. They closed the door so that there would not be any light in the hall and sat back to wait.

Time passed quickly because the gentlemen had lots to talk about. Soon the clock struck midnight. Dr. Classen, who thought the whole ghost story was very funny, smiled. "Perhaps we've frightened the ghost," he said.

"Have patience, my friend," Herr Sesemann replied. "It may come at one o'clock."

But when the clock struck one there was not a sound to be heard. Even the street was ghostly quiet.

Suddenly, the doctor lifted his finger. "Do you hear something?" he whispered.

They listened and heard the bar on the door being pushed back. The key turned twice, and the door was pushed open.

Herr Sesemann reached for the candelabra. "Who is there?" he called as he opened the door. The doctor stood beside him as they stepped into the hall.

Pale moonlight shone in the open door. And there, on the threshold, stood a motionless white form.

As the two men walked forward, the figure turned and gave a little scream. It was Heidi in her white nightgown and bare feet.

"I do believe that is your little Swiss girl," the doctor said. The two men looked at each other in astonishment.

"Heidi, why have you come downstairs? Where are you going?" Herr Sesemann asked.

"I don't know." Heidi shivered in her nightgown. She was as surprised to find herself downstairs as the gentlemen were.

The doctor stepped forward and offered Heidi his hand. "I think I can handle this," he told Herr Sesemann.

"Don't be afraid," he said to Heidi. And he slowly led her up the stairs to her room. The doctor tucked Heidi snugly back into her bed. Soon she had stopped trembling.

"Now that you see everything is all right," the doctor said, "can you tell me where you wanted to go?"

"I didn't want to go anywhere. I was just down there, all at once," Heidi explained.

"Really?" the doctor said kindly. "And

before you were there were you dreaming of anything in particular?"

"Oh, yes," Heidi said. "Every night I dream the same thing. I dream I am with my grandfather, and I can hear the wind in the fir trees outside. It is so beautiful, with the stars sparkling brightly. I run to the door to look out. But when I wake up I am always in Frankfurt." Heidi struggled to swallow the lump in her throat.

"And do you have pain anywhere? In your back or your head?"

"No, only here sometimes." Heidi put her hand on her chest. "Something presses like a big stone."

"So hard that you want to cry out?" the doctor asked.

"Yes," Heidi nodded. "But I don't dare. Fräulein Rottenmeier has forbidden it."

"So you swallow it down until another time," the doctor said thoughtfully. "Heidi, do you like to stay in Frankfurt?"

"Oh, yes," Heidi said. But it sounded more like no.

"Was it unpleasant on the Alm with your grandfather? It's harsh and dreary there, isn't it?"

"Oh, no, it's lovely there," Heidi replied. But she couldn't say anything else. The memory and the excitement were overwhelming, and tears began streaming down her cheeks.

The doctor rubbed Heidi's back. "Go ahead and cry a little," he said. "Then go to sleep and have happy dreams. Tomorrow everything will be all right."

When Heidi had fallen back to sleep, the doctor walked quietly downstairs to the room where Herr Sesemann was waiting. "We've found your ghost," the doctor said. "Your little Heidi walks in her sleep!"

Herr Sesemann was astonished. It was not at all what he had expected. But he was even more alarmed by what the doctor said next.

"The child is so unhappy that she is wasting away from homesickness. And there is just one remedy. You must send her home at once."

Chapter 13

"SLEEPWALKING! Wasting away! Homesick!" Herr Sesemann was very upset. The child was wasting away in his house, and no one had noticed it. "We must do something."

Though it was only beginning to grow light outside, Herr Sesemann called Fräulein Rottenmeier and all of the servants to the dining room. They came down one by one, each looking more terrified than the last. What a relief it was to see Herr Sesemann barking orders in high spirits. He did not look at all as if he'd been frightened by a ghost.

The master of the house asked Fräulein Rottenmeier to get a trunk. She and Tinette were ordered to pack it with all of Heidi's things and some of Klara's things besides.

Sebastian was sent to fetch Heidi's aunt Dete from the house where she worked.

And Johann was to prepare the carriage.

Without explaining anything further, Herr Sesemann left Fräulein Rottenmeier standing openmouthed in the dining room. He hurried up the stairs to talk to his daughter.

Klara had been awakened by the stir in the house. She was already sitting up in bed when her papa came in.

Herr Sesemann explained that the ghost had really been Heidi and that her nightly wanderings were due to homesickness.

Klara did not want Heidi to leave. But she did not want her friend to be sick, either. She agreed that they should send Heidi back to the Alm — but only after her father had promised that she could go visit Heidi on the Alm the following summer.

When Heidi's aunt Dete arrived, Herr

Sesemann told her that he hoped she would take Heidi home that very day. Dete was shocked.

"I hope the child has not done wrong by you," she said.

"Quite the opposite," Herr Sesemann said. "I am afraid we have done wrong by the child. She must return to the Alm for her own health."

Dete was relieved to hear that Heidi had not embarrassed herself. But then she recalled the Alm-Uncle's angry face the last time she had seen him. She remembered his command that she never come before him again. With a shudder she explained that she could not take Heidi home that day or the next.

"Very well," Herr Sesemann said. "Sebastian will take the child home."

In all the hustle and bustle, nobody thought to tell Heidi what was going on. The little girl was waiting in her room to be called down for breakfast. When she finally came downstairs, Herr Sesemann gave her a questioning look.

"Well, little one, what do you say to all of this?" he asked.

Heidi looked at him, confused.

"Why, you don't know anything about it!" Herr Sesemann laughed. "You are going home today, right after breakfast."

"Home?" Heidi whispered. She could not speak aloud, and it was suddenly very difficult to breathe.

"Don't you want to go?" Herr Sesemann asked.

"Oh, yes," Heidi replied. "Yes, I do!"

"Then eat a hearty breakfast," Herr Sesemann said. "Soon you'll be in the carriage and away!"

Heidi could not swallow a mouthful. She was too excited. Herr Sesemann saw that it would be impossible for the girl to get anything down. He told Sebastian to pack a large lunch and excused Heidi to go and talk to Klara before she left.

Heidi's trunk sat in Klara's room. It was packed with lots of new dresses and aprons and underwear. "Look," Klara said, holding up a basket.

Heidi jumped and clapped her hands in delight. The basket was filled with lovely soft white rolls for the grandmother. Klara had not forgotten.

Heidi dashed to her room one last time to take her lovely picture book from under her pillow. She looked into her closet and pulled something from the back corner. Then she wrapped it in her old red kerchief and placed it on top of the basket.

Heidi had to say good-bye to Klara and Herr Sesemann quickly. Sebastian was already waiting in the carriage. When she turned to say good-bye to Fräulein Rottenmeier, the fräulein grabbed the red bundle out of Heidi's basket and threw it on the floor.

"No, Adelheid," she said in her stern

way. "You cannot leave this house looking like an urchin."

Heidi did not dare pick up the bundle. But Herr Sesemann saw that she longed to have it.

"Heidi shall carry home whatever she likes," he said in a decided voice. He handed the parcel back to Heidi.

Heidi thanked Herr Sesemann for the bundle and for everything else he had done. She promised she would think of Klara and her papa often. And most of all she would look forward to seeing them on the Alm soon.

"And please tell the doctor thank you," she said. "He told me everything would be all right in the morning. And it is!"

Klara and Heidi waved to each other until the carriage turned out of sight. Soon Heidi was sitting next to Sebastian on the train with her basket of rolls on her lap. She did not want to let the basket out of her sight. Everything seemed like a dream, and she could not believe that tomorrow she would be able to give the grandmother the rolls herself.

After a while Heidi's eyes closed, and she did not awaken until Sebastian shook her arm.

"Wake up. It is time to get out," he said gently. Already they were in the town where they would spend the night.

The next day Sebastian hired a man with a cart to take Heidi and her trunk to Little Village.

"When you get there, can you take the child up onto the Alm?" Sebastian asked. The man with the cart gave Sebastian a strange look.

"I can walk alone from there," Heidi said. "I know the way to Grandfather's home from Little Village."

Sebastian was not sure he should allow Heidi to travel on alone, but she looked very sure of herself. At last he handed Heidi a letter and a small package from Herr Sesemann.

"Keep them safe, little mam'sell," he said, holding on to her small hand. Heidi promised she would, climbed into the cart, and waved good-bye.

"Aren't you the child who lived with the Alm-Uncle?" the cart man asked as they drove away.

"Yes."

"And did you have a terrible time in Frankfurt?" he asked.

"Oh, no. I had as good a time as anyone can in Frankfurt. But Herr Sesemann allowed me to come home," Heidi replied.

"*Allowed* you to come home?" the cart man asked. "You did not want to stay there?"

"Oh, no," Heidi shook her head. "I would rather be home with my grandfather on the Alm than anywhere else in the world."

As they got closer to Little Village, Heidi

wanted very badly to jump from the cart and run as fast as she could up the hill. When the cart stopped at last and the cart man had lifted her down, she thanked him quickly.

"My grandfather will come for the trunk," she said. Then she turned and made her way toward the mountain path.

Heidi ran as fast as she could. Now and then she had to stop to catch her breath. The basket was heavy, and the path grew steeper with every step.

She had only one thought while she went. Will the grandmother be sitting in the same corner? When Peter's hut was finally in sight, Heidi ran a little faster. When she opened the door and ran into the room, she was breathing so hard she could barely speak.

"Heavens," cried a voice in the corner. "Our Heidi used to run in here like that. If only she were with us now."

"Here I am, Grandmother. Here I am!"

Heidi cried. She rushed into the corner and knelt with her head and arms in the old woman's lap.

The grandmother stroked Heidi's curls, and two tears of joy fell from her blind eyes. "Are you really here, Heidi? Can it be?"

"It's really me, Grandmother," Heidi said. "Don't cry. I am really back and I will come every day and never go away again." Then Heidi began to pile the soft white rolls in the grandmother's lap.

"Oh, child!" the grandmother exclaimed. "What a blessing you have brought me." The grandmother reached out. "Speak again so that I can hear your voice."

Heidi took the book of hymns from the mantel and began to read. Tears flowed from the grandmother's eyes again. "So many blessings," she said. "But the greatest blessing, child, is you."

Chapter 14

HEIDI would have liked to read to the grandmother for hours. But she was eager to go home. She promised she would be back the very next day. Leaving the basket, Heidi took her red parcel, the letter, and the package from Herr Sesemann and continued up the path.

Heidi had not gone very far when she stopped. She removed the fine feathered hat she had worn on her trip from Frankfurt and her fine Sunday dress. Then she opened her red bundle, took out her battered straw hat, and put it on. Wearing just her slip and her old hat, Heidi walked the rest of the way.

Every few steps Heidi had to stop and

look around. The sun was starting to set, and the light was red upon the mountaintops. Everywhere the grass was green, and the valley below was covered in mist. To Heidi it was the most beautiful sight in the whole world.

Soon Heidi could see the tops of the fir trees. Then the roof of the hut. And then the hut itself. And on the seat beside the hut sat her grandfather, smoking his pipe.

Before Grandfather could even see her coming, Heidi rushed up and wrapped her arms around him. All she could say was, "Grandfather!" And she said it again and again.

For the first time in many years the Alm-Uncle's eyes grew moist. He held Heidi at arm's length and looked her over.

"You have come home," he said, wiping his eyes. "You don't look well. Did they send you away?"

"Oh, no," Heidi said. "They were all so kind — most of all Klara and Herr Sesemann. But I could hardly bear being away and wanted so much to come home to you." Heidi gave her grandfather the letter Herr Sesemann had sent and the little package that was filled with money. Grandfather read the letter through without saying a word.

"Here, take this money." Grandfather pressed Herr Sesemann's package into Heidi's hands.

"I don't need it," Heidi said.

"Just put it into the cupboard. You will be able to use it sometime," Grandfather replied.

Heidi skipped into the hut and did as she was told. Then she sat down on her high stool and drank milk from her wooden bowl without stopping. "There is nothing as good as our milk, Grandfather," she said when she set the bowl down.

Suddenly, there was a shrill whistle outside. Heidi shot out the door like lightning. There was the whole flock of goats skipping, jumping, and leaping down from meadow. And Peter was in the middle of them.

"Good evening, Peter!" Heidi called. "Little Bear, Little Swan, do you remember me?"

The goats must have known Heidi's voice, for they came and rubbed their heads against her. Even timid Hopli pushed Turk out of the way to stand closer to Heidi.

Peter stood still on the hill.

"Aren't you going to say hello?" Heidi asked.

"Are you really back?" Peter finally managed to say. "Will you come to the meadow tomorrow?"

"Not tomorrow. Tomorrow I must go see the grandmother. But the next day I'll go," Heidi said.

Peter grinned a huge grin before skipping down the rest of the path. "It's good to have you back!" he called over his shoulder.

Inside the hut Grandfather had made Heidi a new bed in the loft and was just spreading the cover on it. Heidi lay down to try it out and fell fast asleep.

Ten times in the night her grandfather got up to check on Heidi. He'd read in Herr Sesemann's letter that she had been walking in her sleep, and he did not want her to hurt herself. But each time he climbed the ladder Grandfather found Heidi in the loft, sleeping soundly with a smile on her face. Her wandering was finally over. Heidi was home on the Alm.